TALES FROM
THE BACK
PEW

CHURCH HARVEST
MESS-TIVAL

written by **Mike Thaler**   illustrated by **Jared Lee**

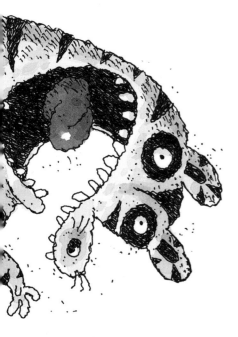

ZONDER**kidz**

ZONDERVAN.com/
AUTHOR**TRACKER**
follow your favorite authors

COOL.

To my beautiful wife, Patty,
who makes every day a festival.
   —M.T.

To Peggy Sheets
   —J.L.

ZONDERKIDZ

Church Harvest Mess-tival
Copyright © 2010 by Mike Thaler
Illustrations © 2010 by Jared Lee Studio, Inc.

Requests for information should be addressed to:

Zonderkidz, *Grand Rapids, Michigan 49530*

Library of Congress Cataloging-in-Publication Data

Thaler, Mike, 1936-
    Church harvest mess-tival / by Mike Thaler ; illustrated by Jared Lee.
       p. cm. — (Tales from the back pew)
       Summary: A boy who loves to celebrate Halloween discovers the fun of attending a
    church party, instead, dressed as a Biblical character.
       ISBN 978-0-310-71595-5 (saddle stitch) [1. Halloween—Fiction. 2. Parties—Fiction. 3.
    Christian life—Fiction.] I. Lee, Jared D., ill. II. Title.
    PZ7.T3Cf 2010
    [E]—dc22   2008037328

Editor: Mary Hassinger
Art director: Merit Kathan

Printed in China

10 11 12 13 14 /LPC/ 6 5 4 3 2 1

It's Halloween! But Mom says I can't go trick-or-treating.

I can't even dress up like a monster or a maniac.

 Nothing weird, wild, or wacky.

No ghouls, goblins, or gore. No fins, fangs, or fur.

No skulls or screams or scary things at all. Boring!
What's October without shock-tober?

She says I have to go to the church party dressed like a Bible character. Boring!

It's called a harvest festival. I'd rather go to a horror festerval.

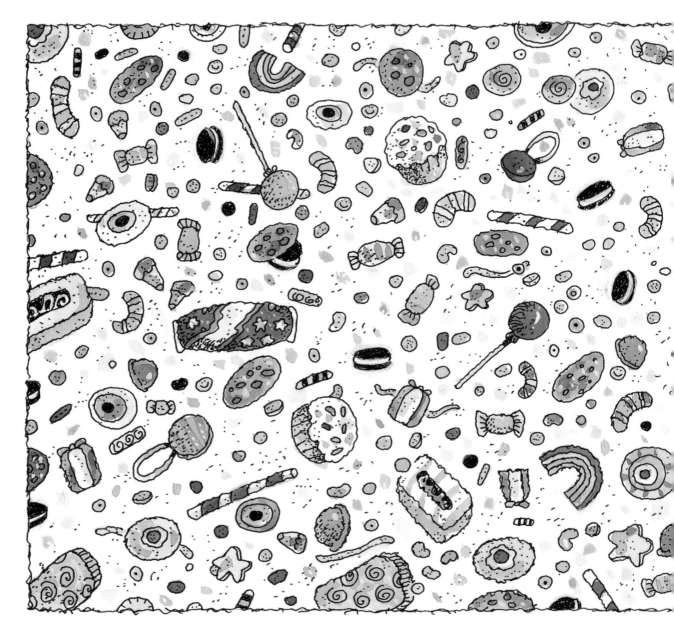

 And what about candy? I won't be able to collect a giant, globby, gooey glump of guaranteed sugar shock.

Instead of shouting boo,

I'll be sitting in a pew.

I'll be at church with a bunch of angels. No fun, no fiends, no frenzy.

Mom says it'll be fun, but first we have to make a costume. She says I could be Noah and bring my two gerbils. Or Joshua and toot a horn.

I'd rather wear a horn.

She says I can be Moses and wear a beard.

Maybe I can wear it on my forehead and be a *little* weird.
Mom says to keep my chin up, and we'll have lots of fun.

She says there's lots of games, and you can win lots of candy.

She says there's a basketball shoot, a trumpet toot, throwing hoops...

hurling rings, spinning swings,

bouncing high, eating pie...

painting faces, having races.

Nothing boney, but you can ride a pony.

Nothing sinister, but you can try to dunk the minister.

← PREACHER CREATURE

Hey, maybe it won't be so bad after all. Mom says knowing God is fun. And he'll help me find my costume. So I open up the Bible, and God gives me a whale of an idea!

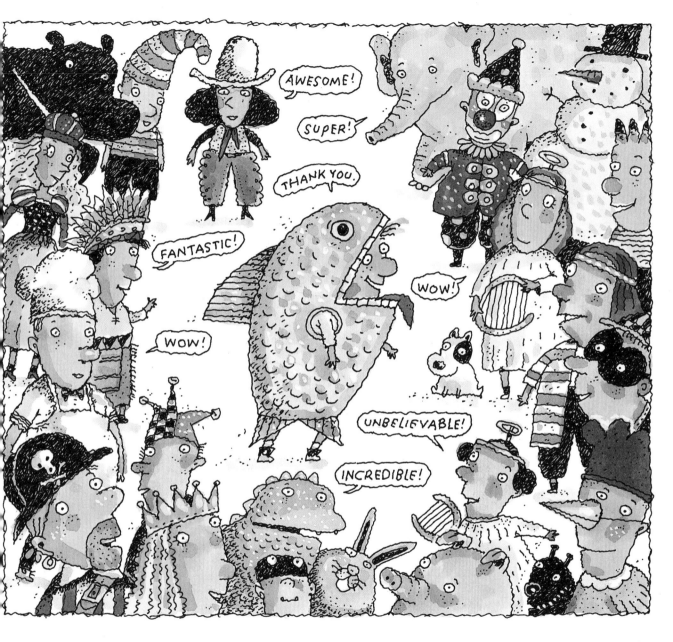

I'll make a big fish and go as Jonah. God is good *all* the time!
Even on Halloween.

He will yet fill
your mouth with laughter
and your lips with shouts of joy.
—Job 8:21

304.3